AVENGERS K #7
ASSEMBLING THE AVENGERS

S.H.I.E.L.D. Agent Natasha Romanoff, A.K.A. the Black Widow, is tasked with preventing Gen. Thaddeus "Thunderbolt" Ross from capturing the Hulk. She arrives in New York City to find a massive battle between the Hulk and the Abomination, and encounters a gamma-irradiated Dr. Samuel Sterns. With gods and monsters walking the Earth, is it time for S.H.I.E.L.D. to change?

JIM ZUB
SCRIPT

WOO BIN CHOI WITH **JAE SUNG LEE**
ART

MIN JU LEE
INKS

JAE WOONG LEE, HEE YE CHO & **IN YOUNG LEE**
COLORS

VC's CORY PETIT
LETTERS

WOO BIN CHOI WITH **JAE SUNG LEE, MIN JU LEE, JAE WOONG LEE** & **HEE YE CHO**
COVER ART

Adapted from *MARVEL'S AVENGERS PRELUDE: FURY'S BIG WEEK #1-4*.
Adaptations written by SI YEON PARK and translated by JI EUN PARK

AVENGERS created by STAN LEE and JACK KIRBY

Original comics written by CHRIS YOST and ERIC PEARSON,
and illustrated by LUKE ROSS, DANIEL HDR, AGUSTIN PADILLA, DON HO,
WELLINTON ALVES, RICK KETCHAM, MARK PENNINGTON and CHRIS SOTOMAYOR

Editor SARAH BRUNSTAD
Manager, Licensed Publishing JEFF REINGOLD
VP Brand Management & Development, Asia C.B. CEBULSKI
VP Production & Special Projects JEFF YOUNGQUIST
SVP Print, Sales & Marketing DAVID GABRIEL
Associate Manager, Digital Assets JOE HOCHSTEIN
Associate Managing Editor KATERI WOODY
Assistant Editor CAITLIN O'CONNELL
Senior Editor, Special Projects JENNIFER GRÜNWALD
Editor, Special Projects MARK D. BEAZLEY
Book Designer: ADAM DEL RE

Editor In Chief AXEL ALONSO
Chief Creative Officer JOE QUESADA
President DAN BUCKLEY
Executive Producer ALAN FINE

Spotlight

AVENGERS ACTIVE ROSTER

THOR
Real Name:
THOR ODINSON

HAWKEYE
Real Name:
CLINT BARTON

BLACK WIDOW
Real Name:
NATASHA ROMANOFF

IRON MAN
Real Name:
ANTHONY EDWARD STARK

CAPTAIN AMERICA
Real Name: STEVEN ROGERS

NICK FURY

HULK
Real Name:
ROBERT BRUCE BANNER

EXTRAORDINARY ALLIES

PHIL COULSON

WAR MACHINE

JANE FOSTER

AVENGERS MOST WANTED

WHIPLASH

LOKI

DESTROYER

ABOMINATION

SAMUEL STERNS

ABDOPUBLISHING.COM

Reinforced library bound edition published in 2018 by Spotlight, a division of ABDO, PO Box 398166, Minneapolis, Minnesota 55439. Spotlight produces high-quality reinforced library bound editions for schools and libraries. Published by agreement with Marvel Characters, Inc. Printed in the United States of America, North Mankato, Minnesota.
092017   012018

MARVEL
marvelkids.com
© 2018 MARVEL

THIS BOOK CONTAINS RECYCLED MATERIALS

PUBLISHER'S CATALOGING-IN-PUBLICATION DATA

Names: Zub, Jim, author. | Choi, Woo Bin; Lee, Jae Sung; Lee, Min Ju; Lee, Jae Woong; Cho, Hee Ye; Lee, In Young, illustrators.
Title: Assembling the Avengers / writer: Jim Zub ; art: Woo Bin Choi; Jae Sung Lee; Min Ju Lee; Jae Woong Lee; Hee Ye Cho; In Young Lee.
Description: Minneapolis, MN : Spotlight, 2018 | Series: Avengers K Set 3
Summary: With a changing world full of threats bigger than he could imagine, S.H.I.E.L.D. director Nick Fury struggles to follow orders from the World Security Council. He calls upon Agent Coulson, Hawkeye, and Black Widow for aid to search for the missing Captain America, help Tony Stark fix his failing arc reactor in his chest, stop the Hulk from going on a rampage, and unearth an alien object, followed shortly by its electrifying owner.
Identifiers: LCCN 2017941923 | ISBN 9781532141478 (v.1 ; lib. bdg.) | ISBN 9781532141485 (v.2 ; lib. bdg.) | ISBN 9781532141492 (v.3 ; lib. bdg.) | ISBN 9781532141508 (v.4 ; lib. bdg.) | ISBN 9781532141515 (v.5 ; lib. bdg.) | ISBN 9781532141522 (v.6 ; lib. bdg.) | ISBN 9781532141539 (v.7 ; lib.bdg.)
Subjects: LCSH: Avengers (ficitious character)--Juvenile fiction. | Super heroes--Juvenile fiction. | Graphic Novels--Juvenile fiction. | Media Tie-in--Juvenile fiction.
Classification: DDC 741.5--dc23
LC record available at http://lccn.loc.gov/2017941923

ABDO
Spotlight

A Division of ABDO
abdopublishing.com

"NICK FURY: THE AVENGERS INITIATIVE"

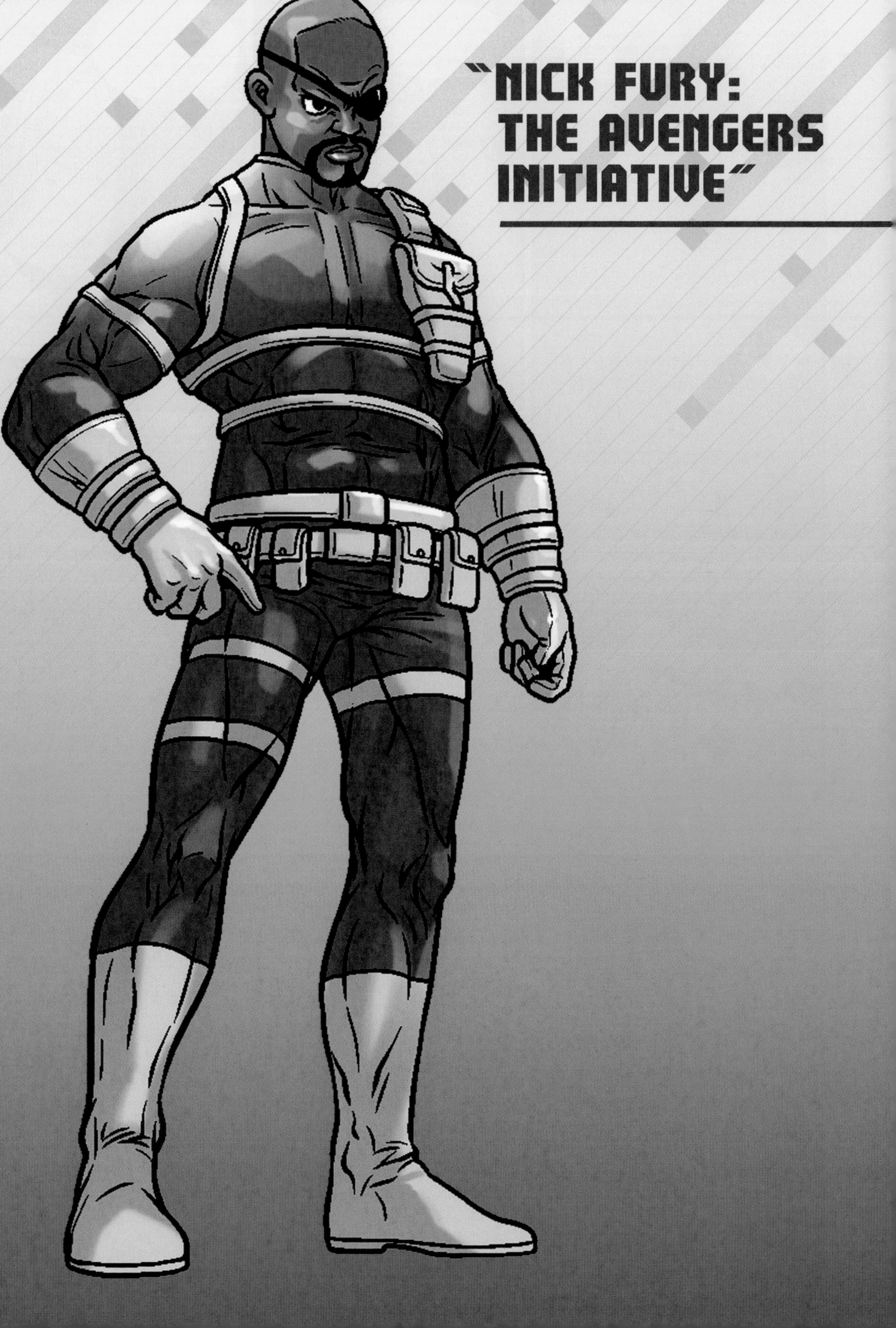

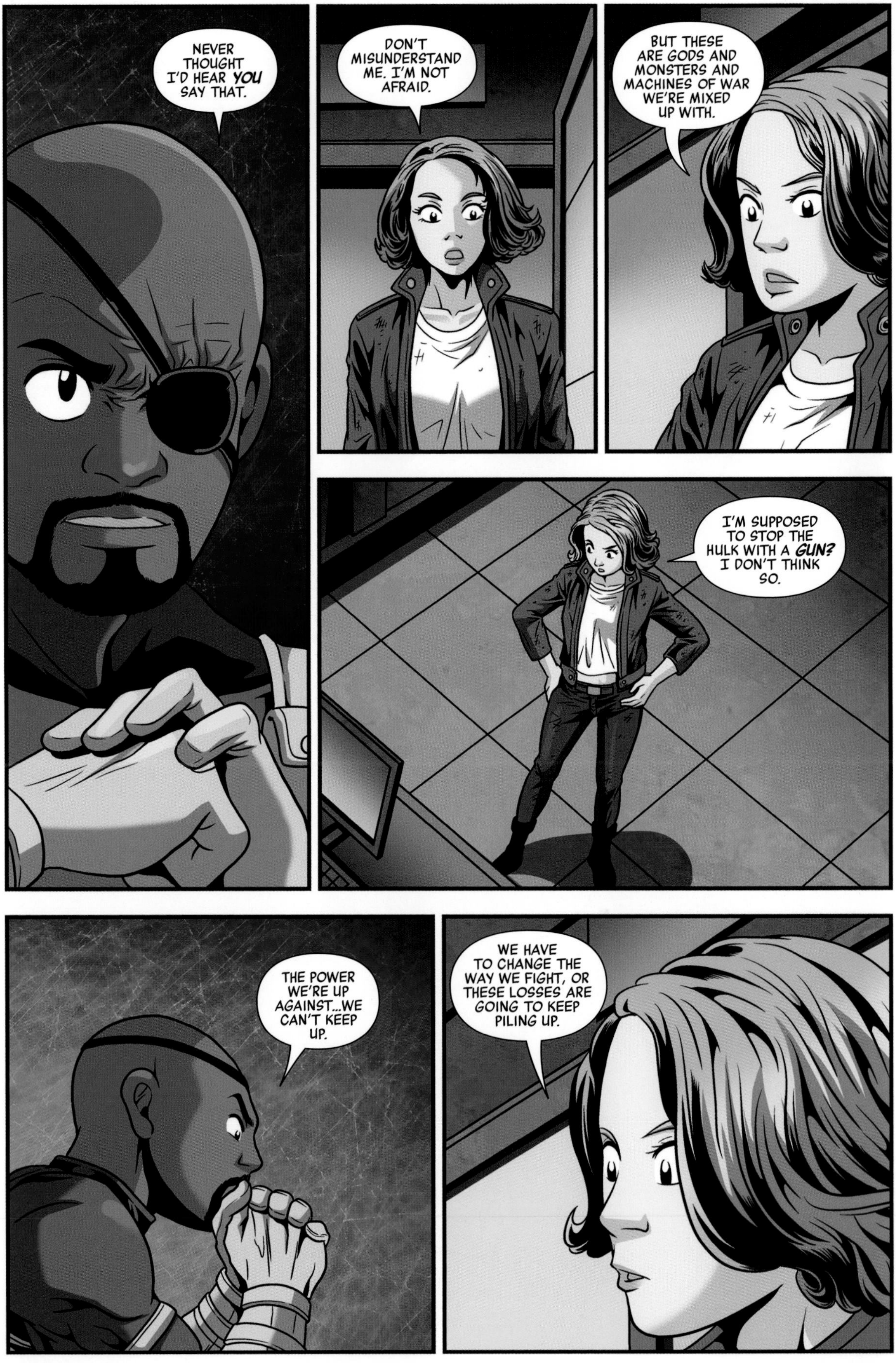
NEVER THOUGHT I'D HEAR YOU SAY THAT.
DON'T MISUNDERSTAND ME. I'M NOT AFRAID.
BUT THESE ARE GODS AND MONSTERS AND MACHINES OF WAR WE'RE MIXED UP WITH.
I'M SUPPOSED TO STOP THE HULK WITH A GUN? I DON'T THINK SO.
THE POWER WE'RE UP AGAINST...WE CAN'T KEEP UP.
WE HAVE TO CHANGE THE WAY WE FIGHT, OR THESE LOSSES ARE GOING TO KEEP PILING UP.

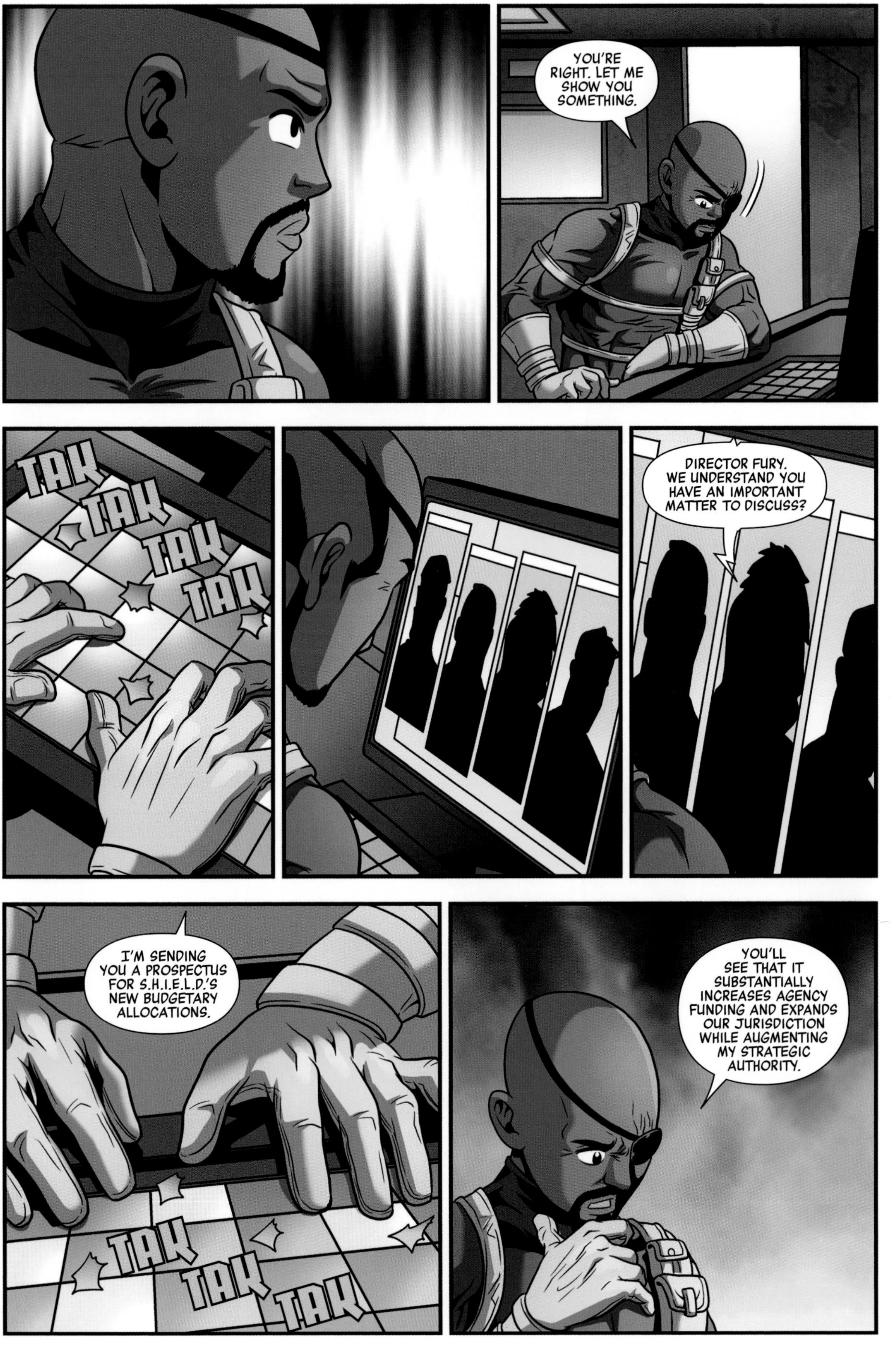
YOU'RE RIGHT. LET ME SHOW YOU SOMETHING.
TAK TAK TAK TAK
DIRECTOR FURY. WE UNDERSTAND YOU HAVE AN IMPORTANT MATTER TO DISCUSS?
I'M SENDING YOU A PROSPECTUS FOR S.H.I.E.L.D.'S NEW BUDGETARY ALLOCATIONS.
TAK TAK TAK
YOU'LL SEE THAT IT SUBSTANTIALLY INCREASES AGENCY FUNDING AND EXPANDS OUR JURISDICTION WHILE AUGMENTING MY STRATEGIC AUTHORITY.

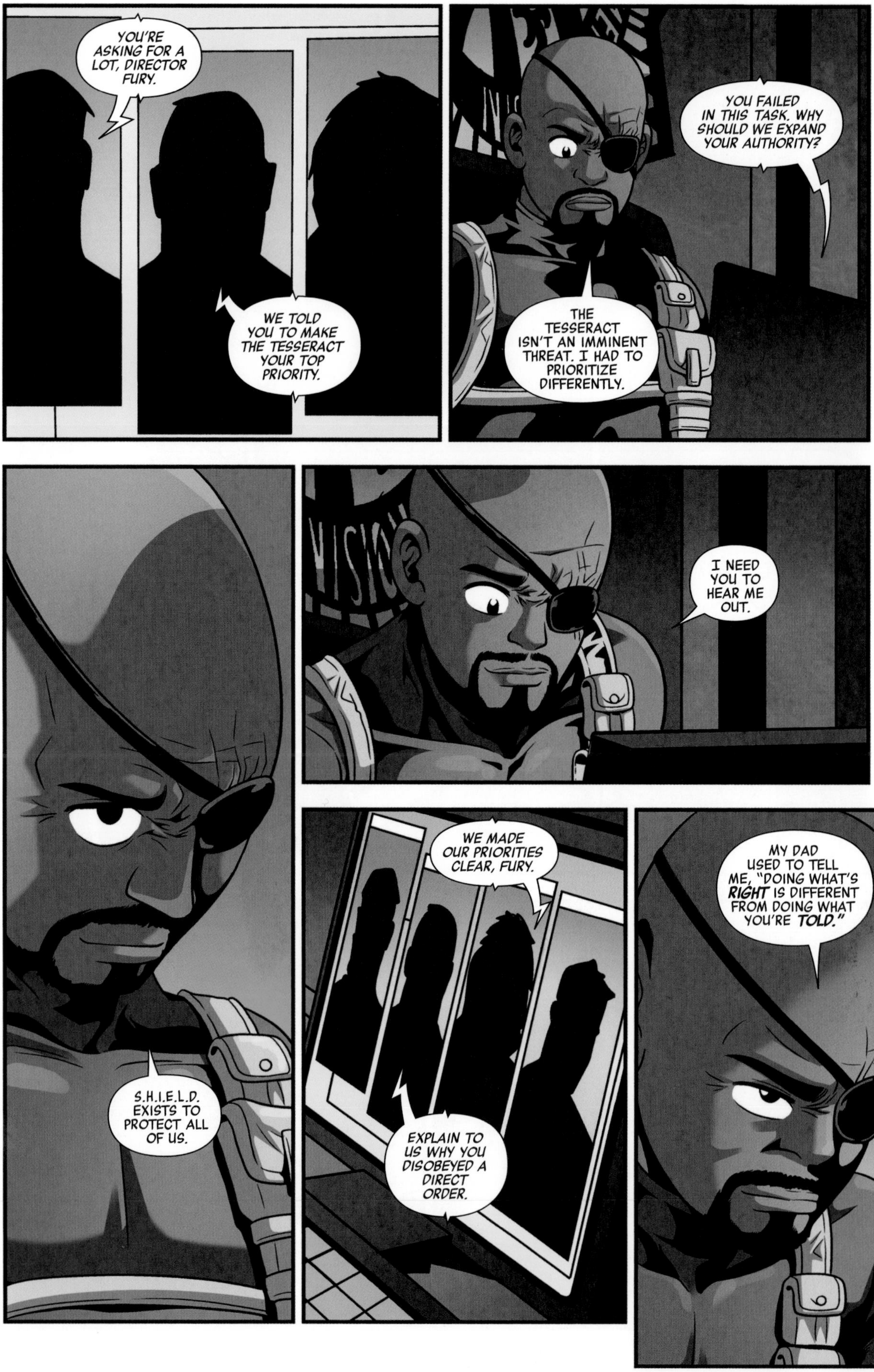

YOU'RE ASKING FOR A LOT, DIRECTOR FURY.
WE TOLD YOU TO MAKE THE TESSERACT YOUR TOP PRIORITY.
YOU FAILED IN THIS TASK. WHY SHOULD WE EXPAND YOUR AUTHORITY?
THE TESSERACT ISN'T AN IMMINENT THREAT. I HAD TO PRIORITIZE DIFFERENTLY.
S.H.I.E.L.D. EXISTS TO PROTECT ALL OF US.
I NEED YOU TO HEAR ME OUT.
WE MADE OUR PRIORITIES CLEAR, FURY.
EXPLAIN TO US WHY YOU DISOBEYED A DIRECT ORDER.
MY DAD USED TO TELL ME, "DOING WHAT'S RIGHT IS DIFFERENT FROM DOING WHAT YOU'RE TOLD."

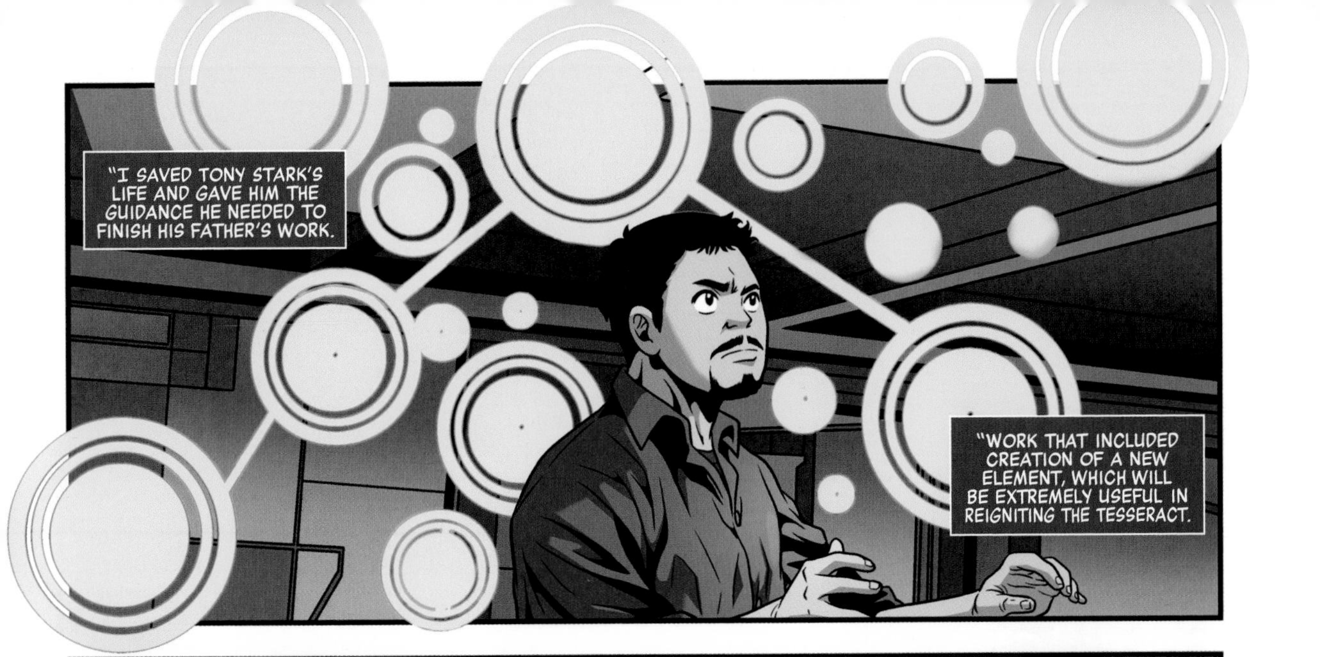
"I SAVED TONY STARK'S LIFE AND GAVE HIM THE GUIDANCE HE NEEDED TO FINISH HIS FATHER'S WORK.
"WORK THAT INCLUDED CREATION OF A NEW ELEMENT, WHICH WILL BE EXTREMELY USEFUL IN REIGNITING THE TESSERACT.

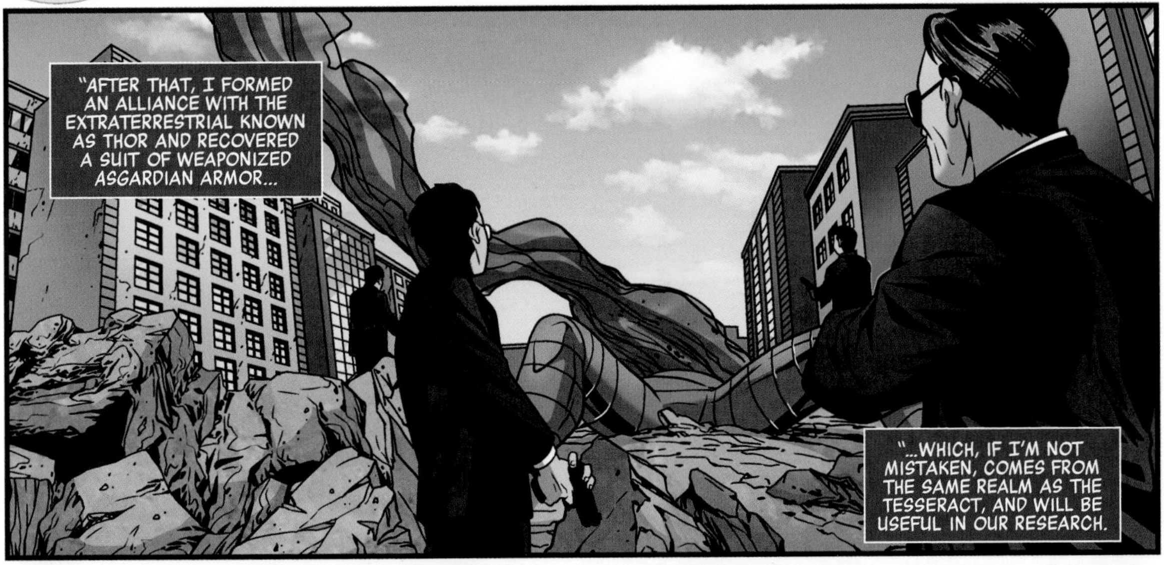
"AFTER THAT, I FORMED AN ALLIANCE WITH THE EXTRATERRESTRIAL KNOWN AS THOR AND RECOVERED A SUIT OF WEAPONIZED ASGARDIAN ARMOR...
"...WHICH, IF I'M NOT MISTAKEN, COMES FROM THE SAME REALM AS THE TESSERACT, AND WILL BE USEFUL IN OUR RESEARCH.

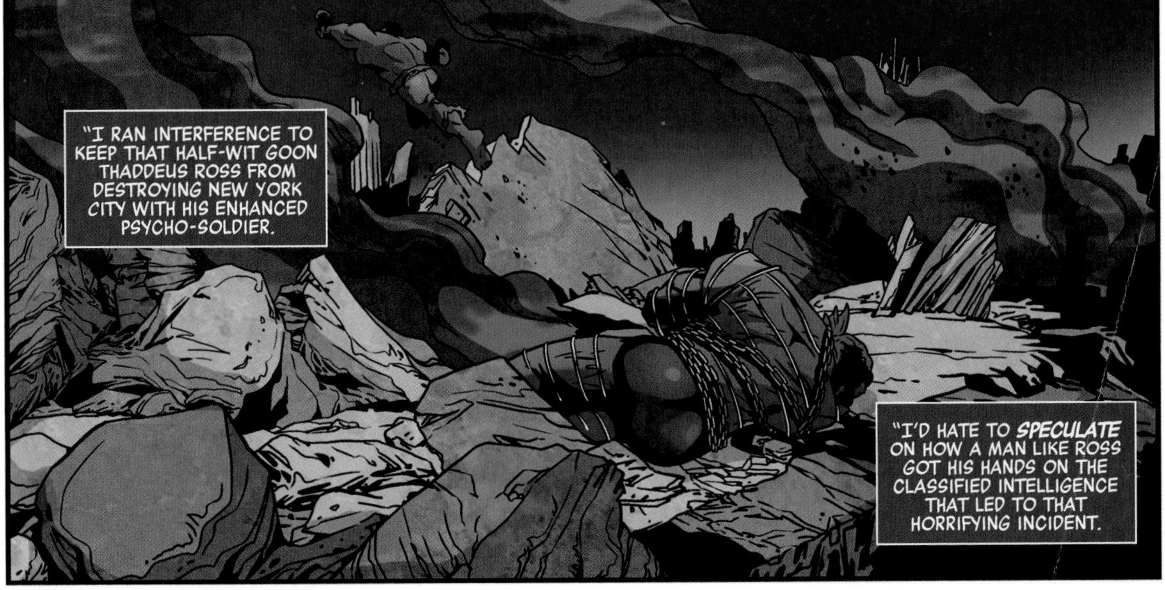
"I RAN INTERFERENCE TO KEEP THAT HALF-WIT GOON THADDEUS ROSS FROM DESTROYING NEW YORK CITY WITH HIS ENHANCED PSYCHO-SOLDIER.
"I'D HATE TO *SPECULATE* ON HOW A MAN LIKE ROSS GOT HIS HANDS ON THE CLASSIFIED INTELLIGENCE THAT LED TO THAT HORRIFYING INCIDENT.

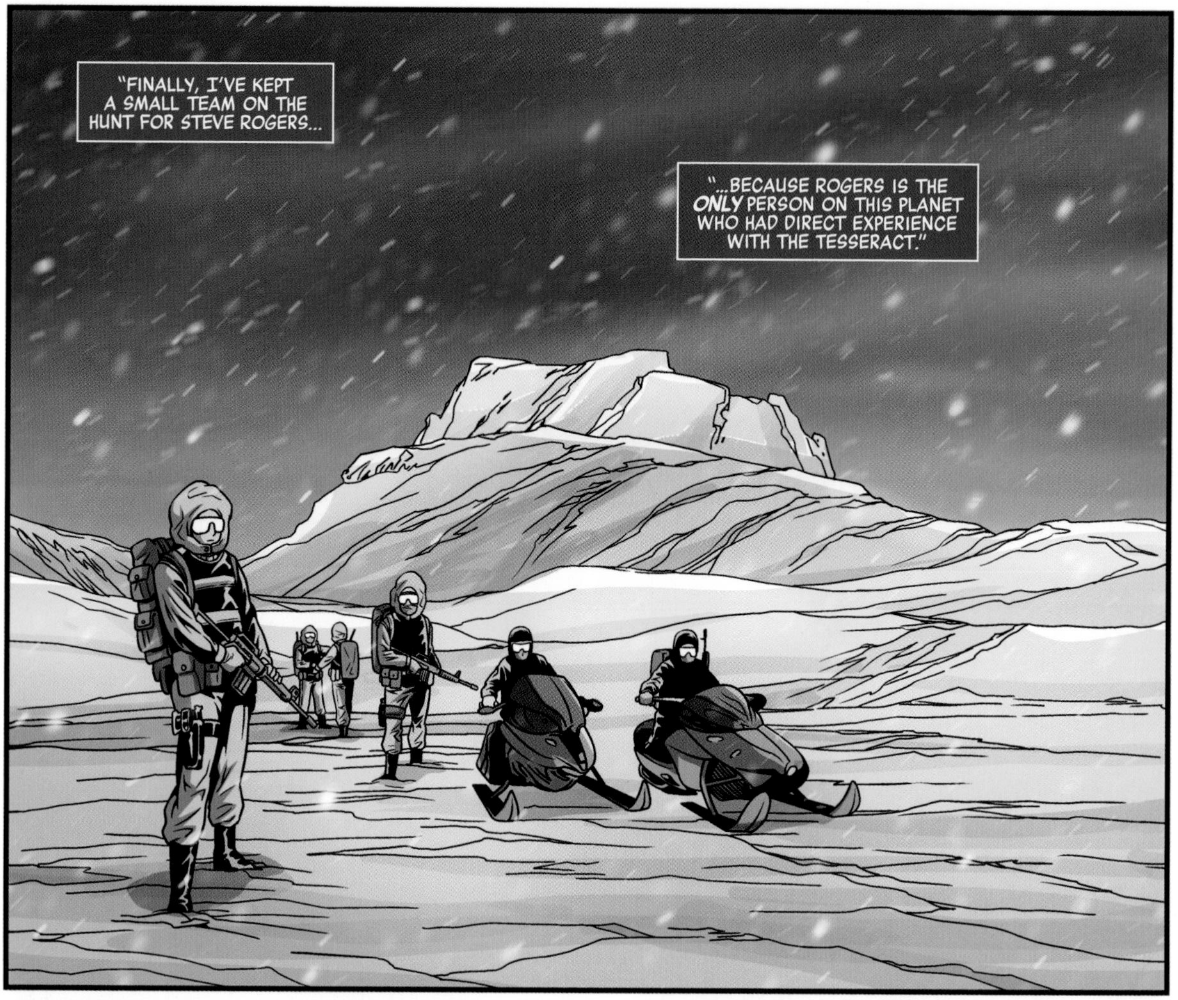
"FINALLY, I'VE KEPT A SMALL TEAM ON THE HUNT FOR STEVE ROGERS...
"...BECAUSE ROGERS IS THE *ONLY* PERSON ON THIS PLANET WHO HAD DIRECT EXPERIENCE WITH THE TESSERACT."

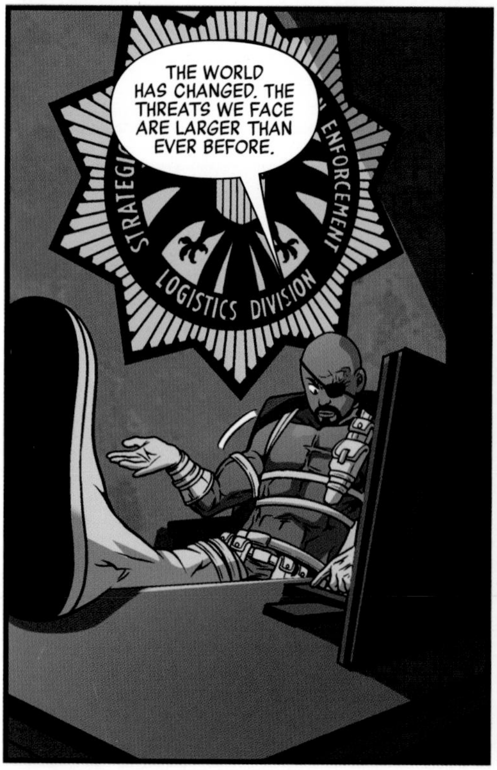
THE WORLD HAS CHANGED. THE THREATS WE FACE ARE LARGER THAN EVER BEFORE.
ENFORCEMENT
LOGISTICS DIVISION

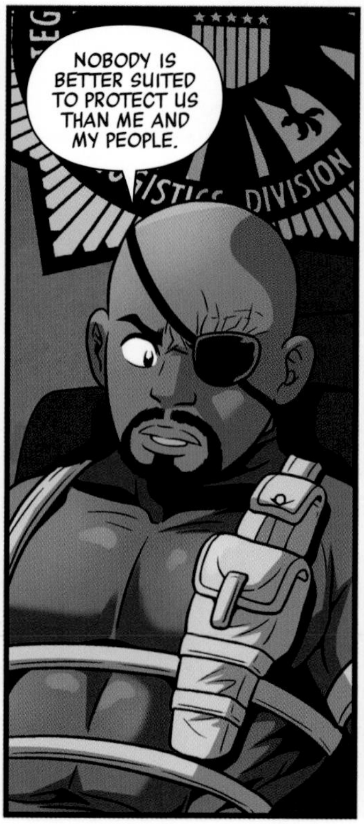
NOBODY IS BETTER SUITED TO PROTECT US THAN ME AND MY PEOPLE.

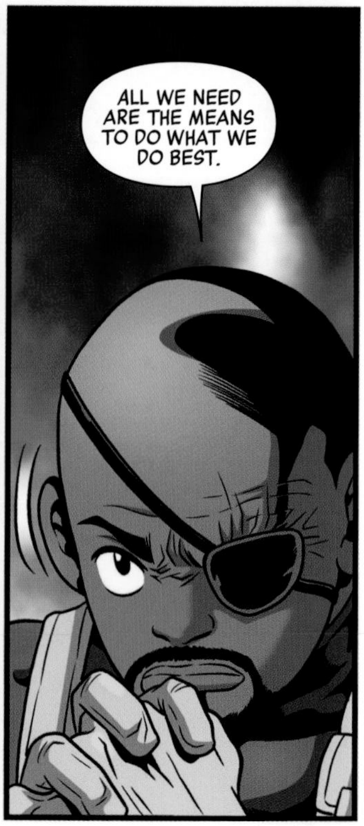
ALL WE NEED ARE THE MEANS TO DO WHAT WE DO BEST.

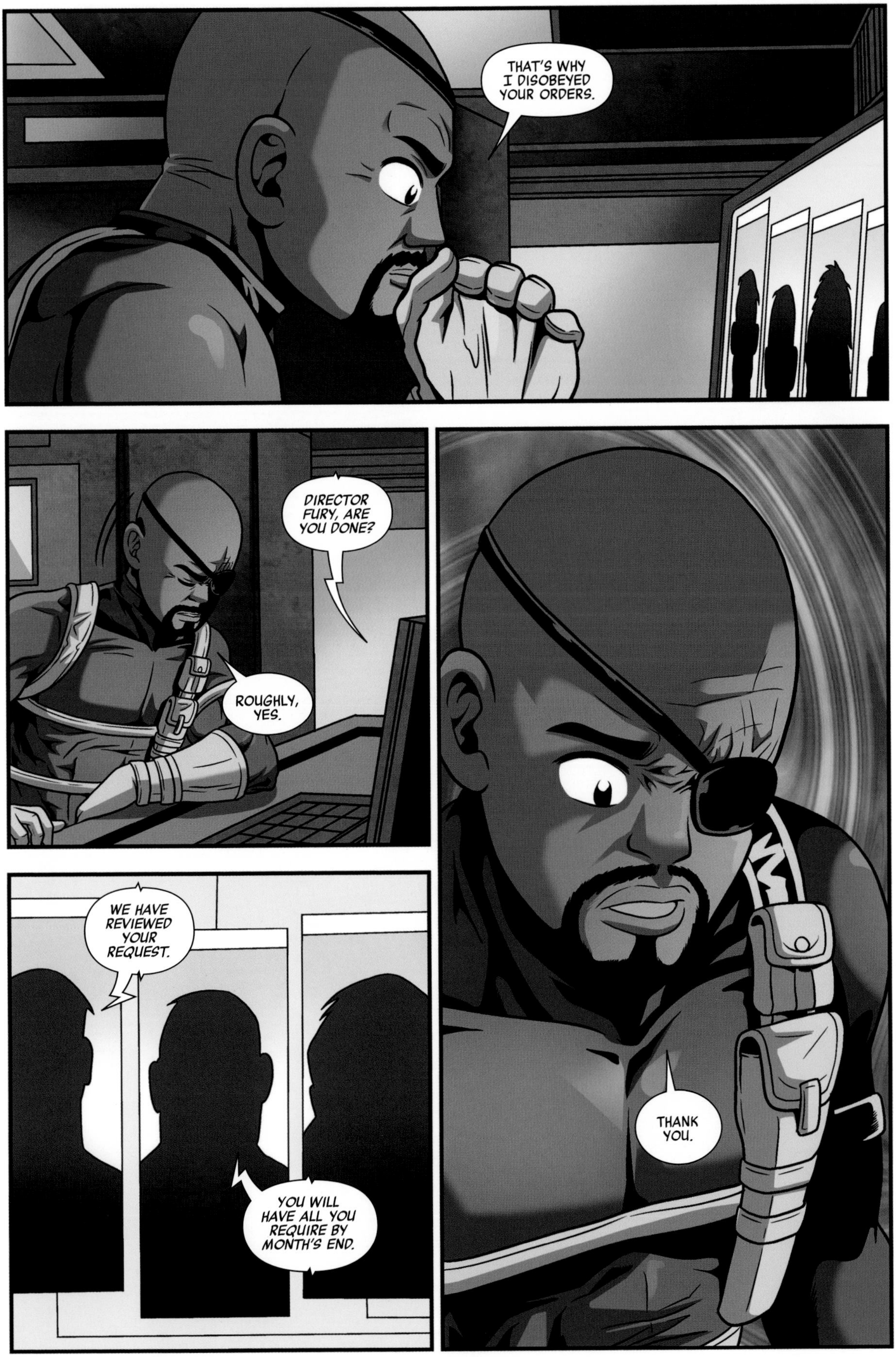
THAT'S WHY I DISOBEYED YOUR ORDERS.
DIRECTOR FURY, ARE YOU DONE?
ROUGHLY, YES.
WE HAVE REVIEWED YOUR REQUEST.
YOU WILL HAVE ALL YOU REQUIRE BY MONTH'S END.
THANK YOU.

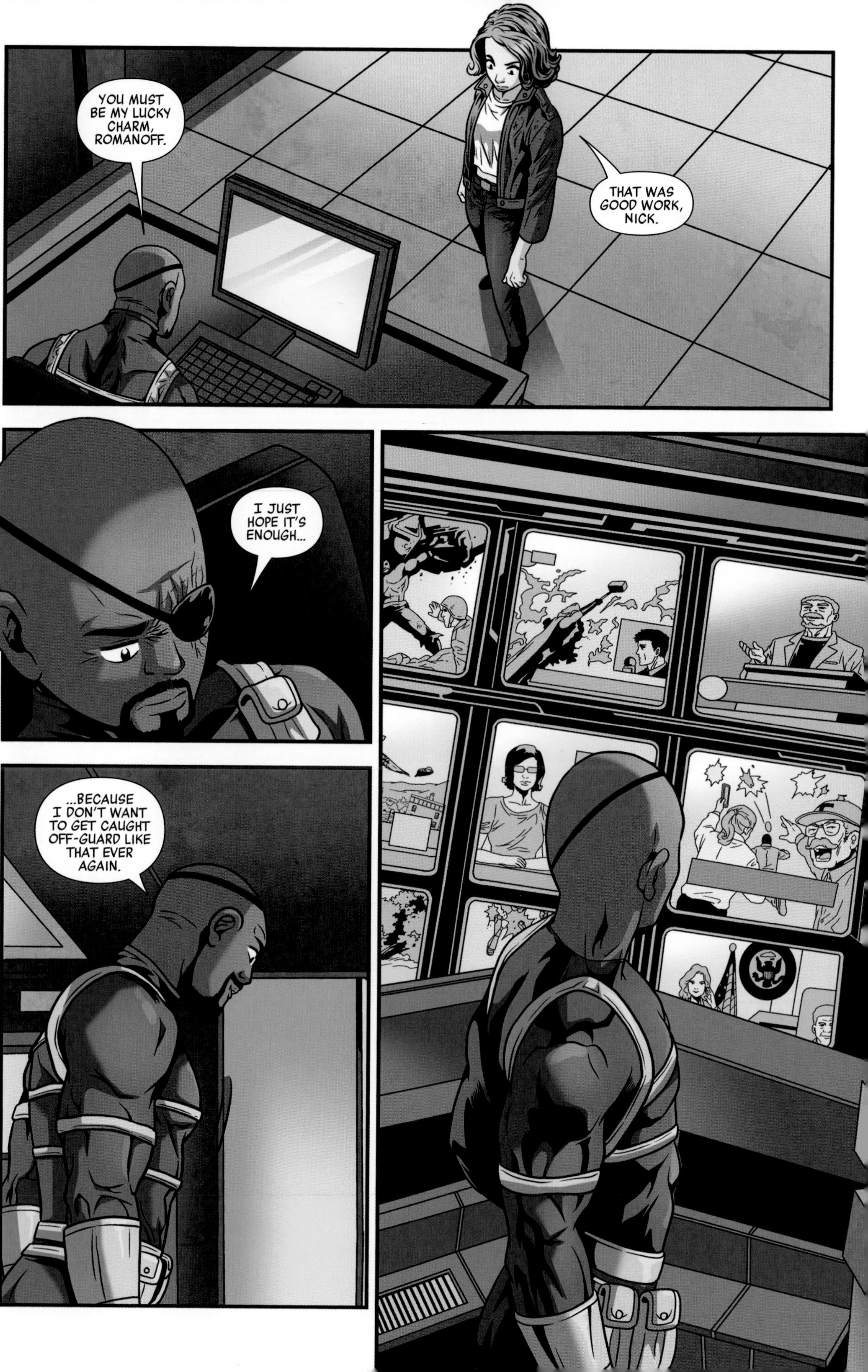
YOU MUST BE MY LUCKY CHARM, ROMANOFF.
THAT WAS GOOD WORK, NICK.
I JUST HOPE IT'S ENOUGH...
...BECAUSE I DON'T WANT TO GET CAUGHT OFF-GUARD LIKE THAT EVER AGAIN.

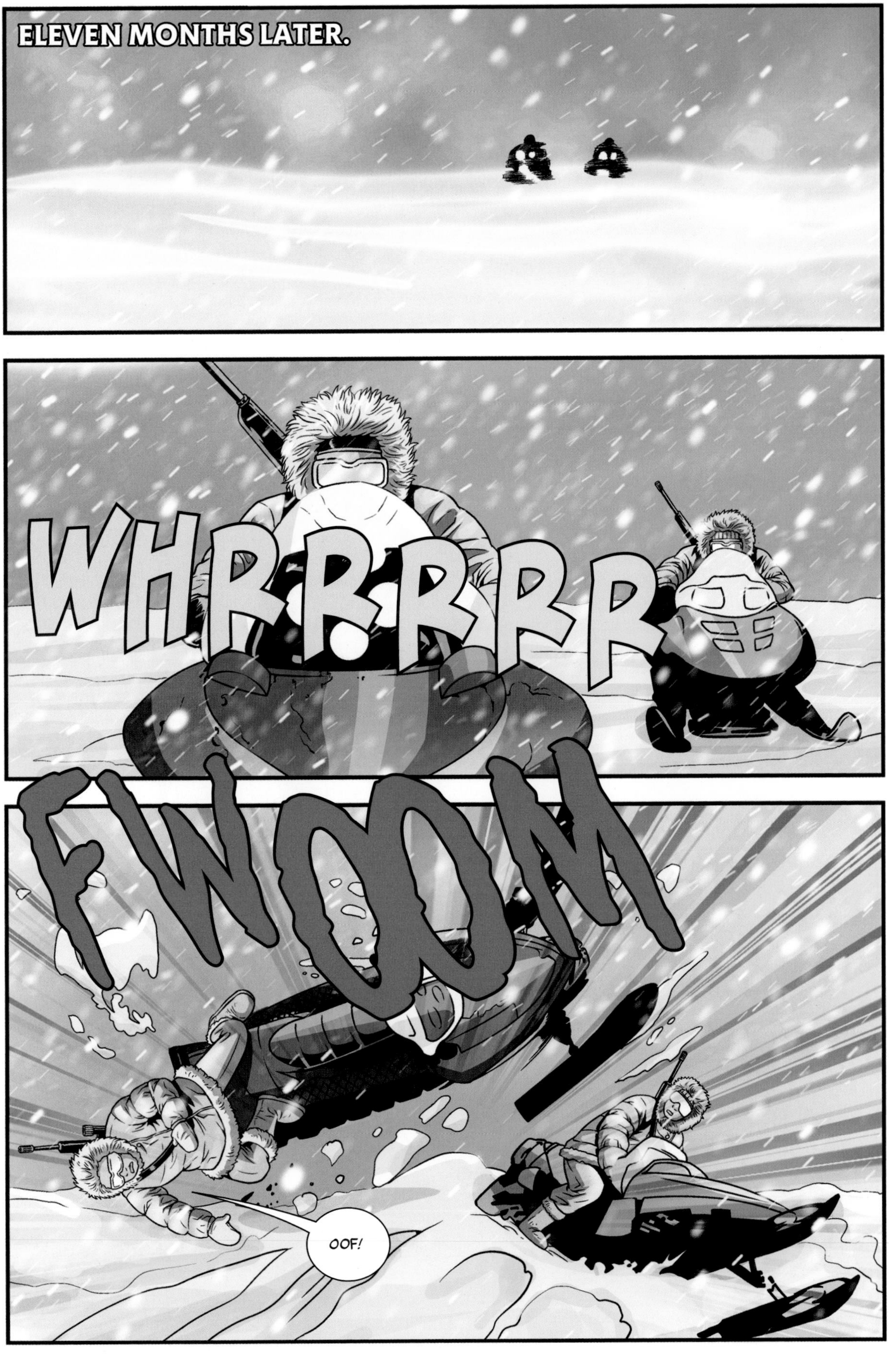
ELEVEN MONTHS LATER.
WHRRRRR
FWOOM
OOF!

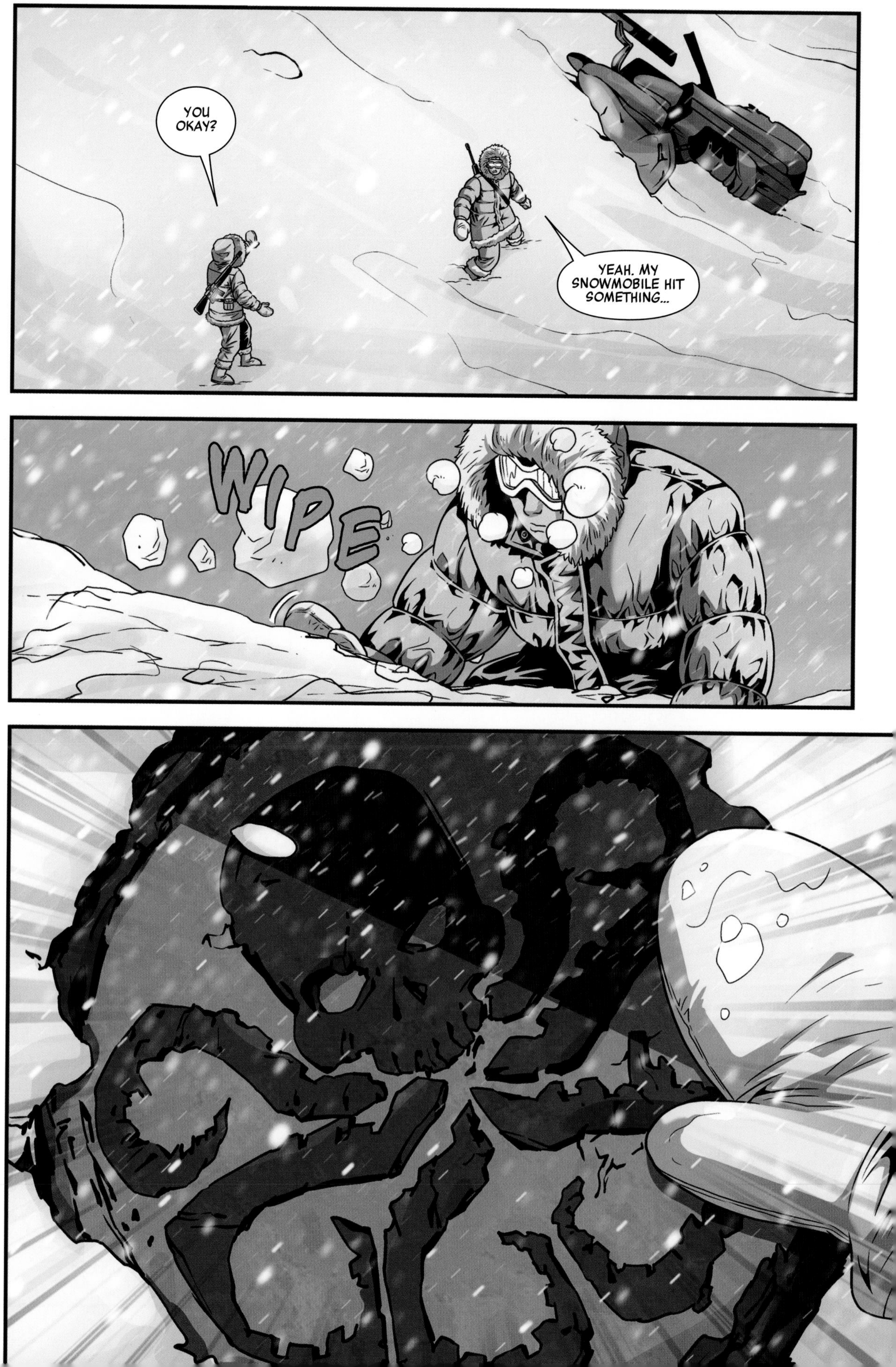

YOU OKAY?
YEAH. MY SNOWMOBILE HIT SOMETHING...
WIPE

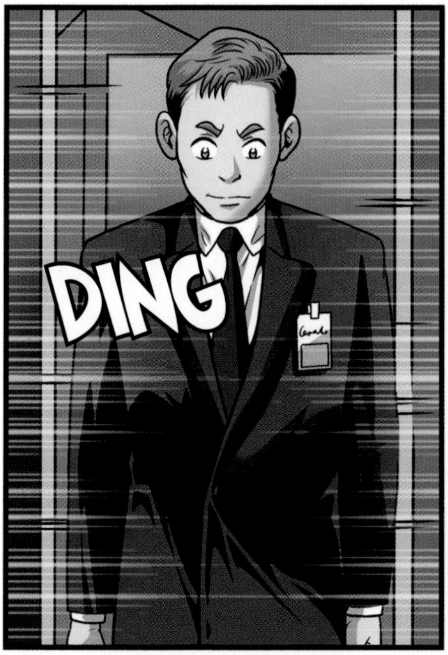
DING

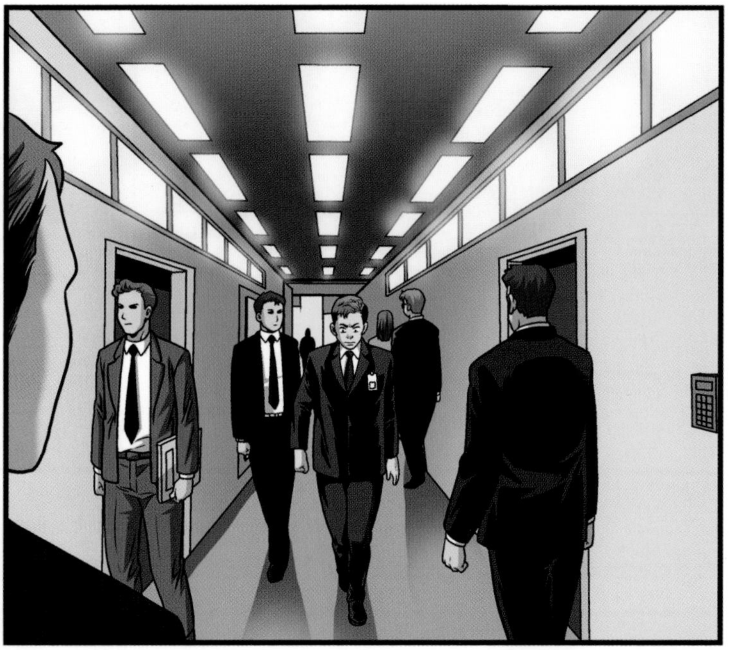

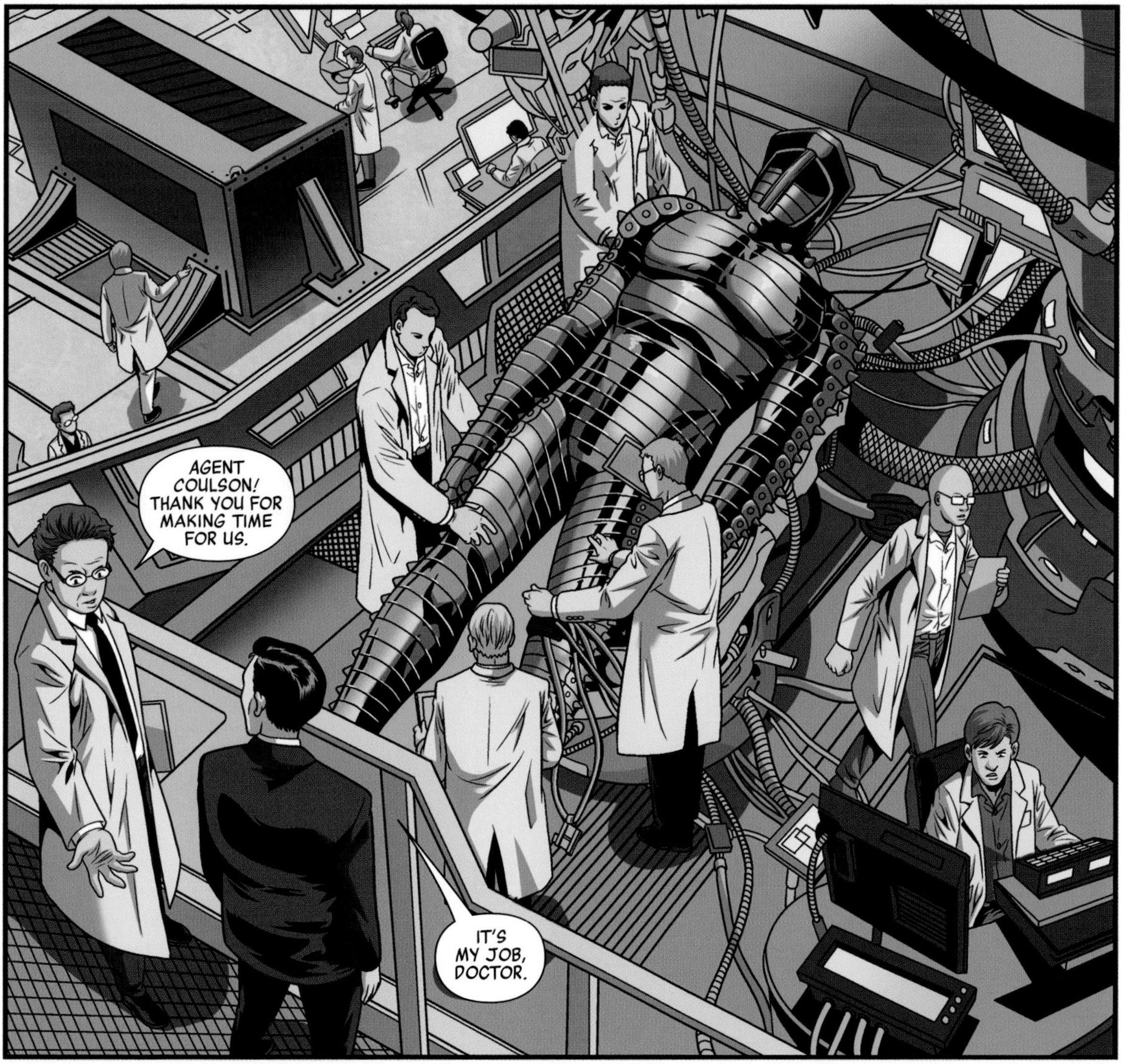
AGENT COULSON! THANK YOU FOR MAKING TIME FOR US.
IT'S MY JOB, DOCTOR.

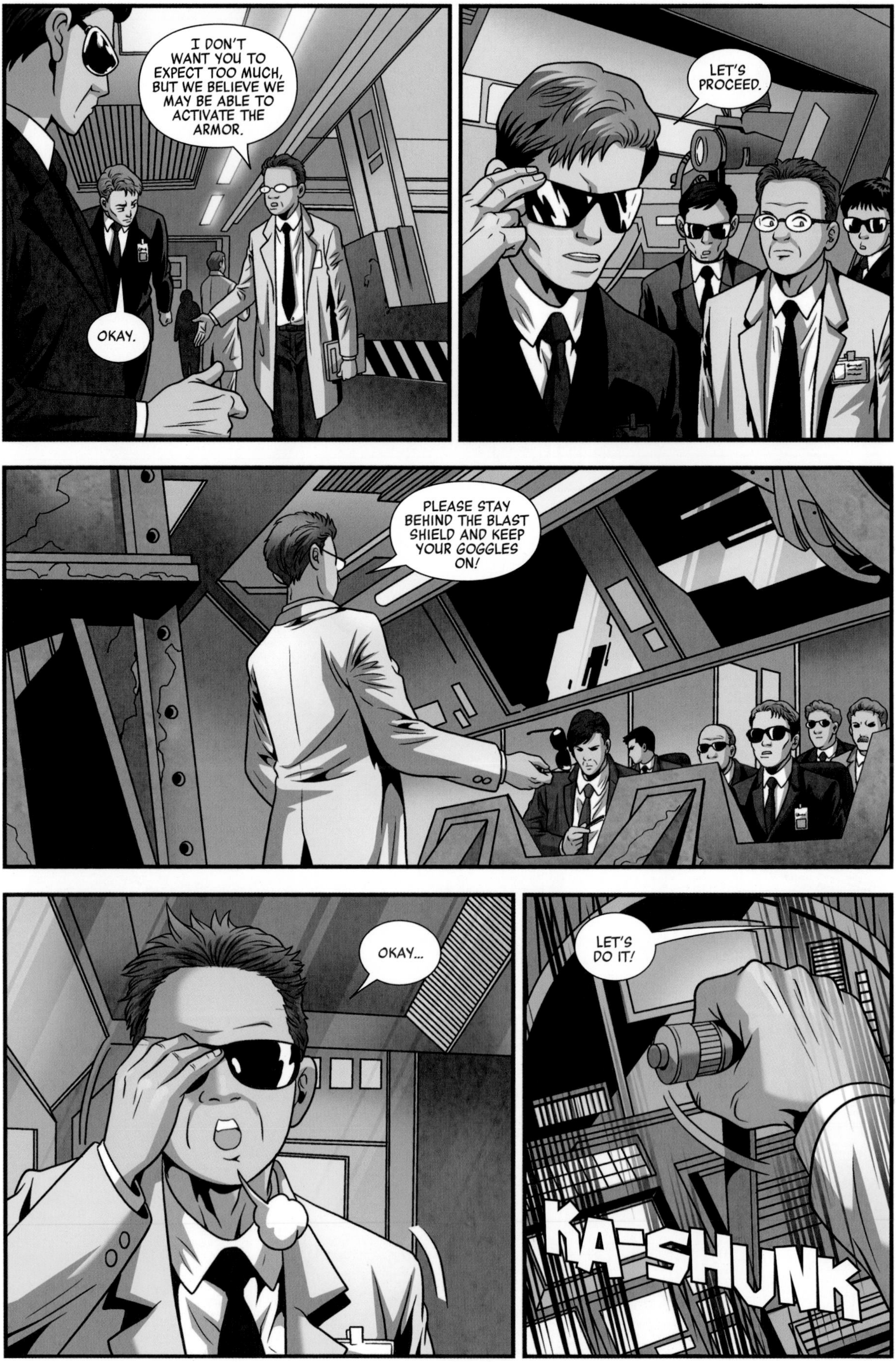
I DON'T WANT YOU TO EXPECT TOO MUCH, BUT WE BELIEVE WE MAY BE ABLE TO ACTIVATE THE ARMOR.
OKAY.
LET'S PROCEED.
PLEASE STAY BEHIND THE BLAST SHIELD AND KEEP YOUR GOGGLES ON!
OKAY...
LET'S DO IT!
KA-SHUNK

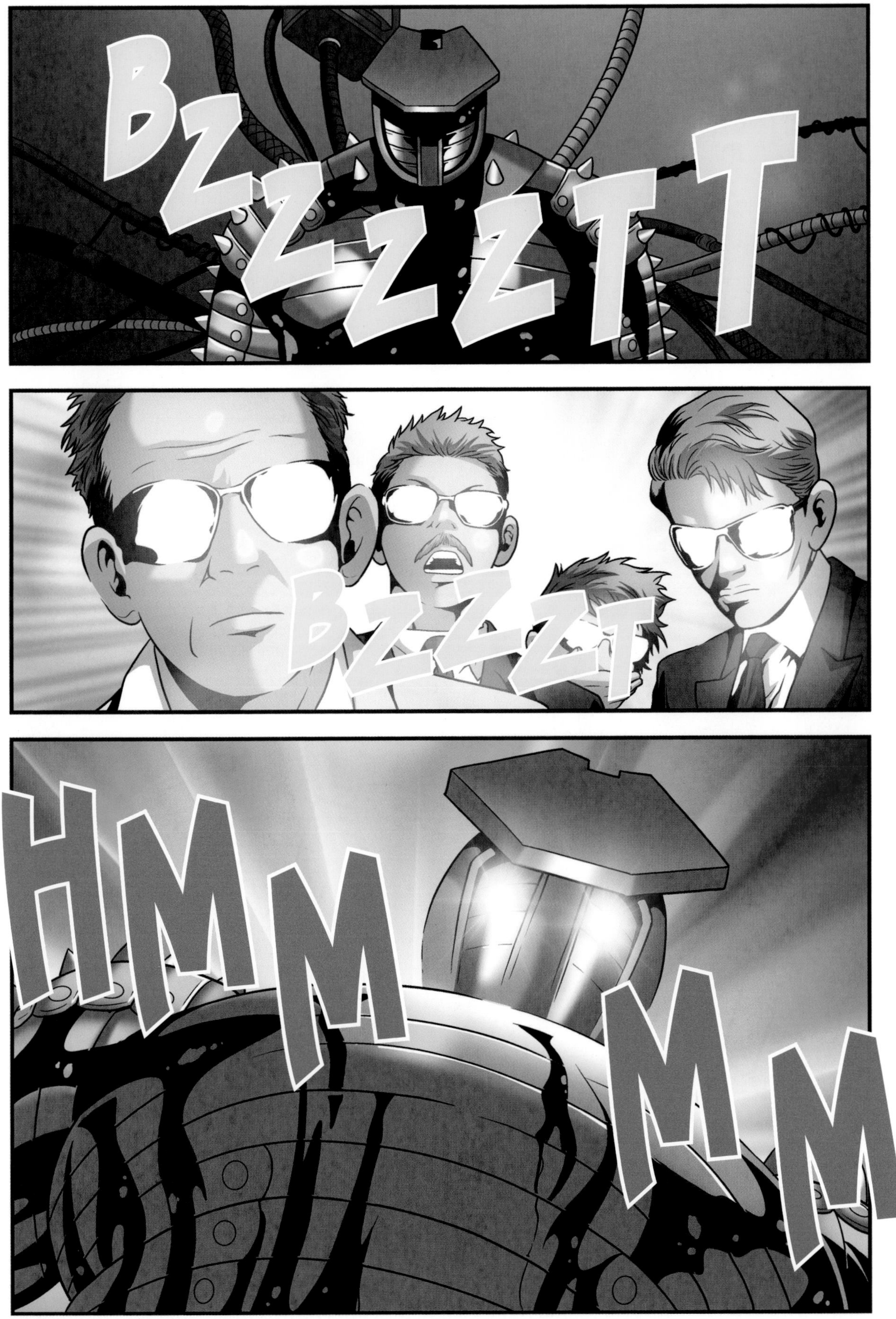
BZZZZTT
BZZZT
HMMMM

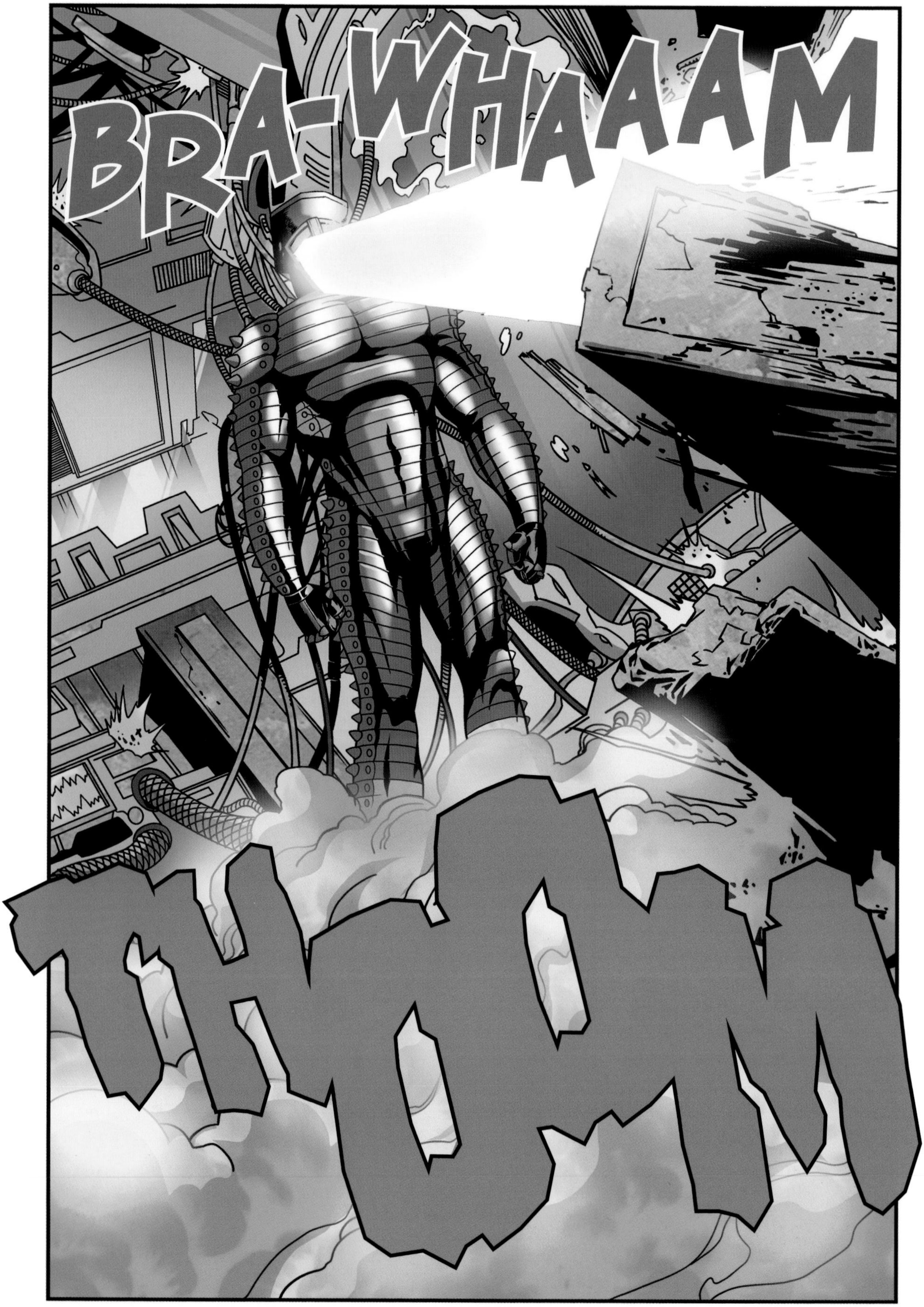
BRA-WHAAAAM
THOOM

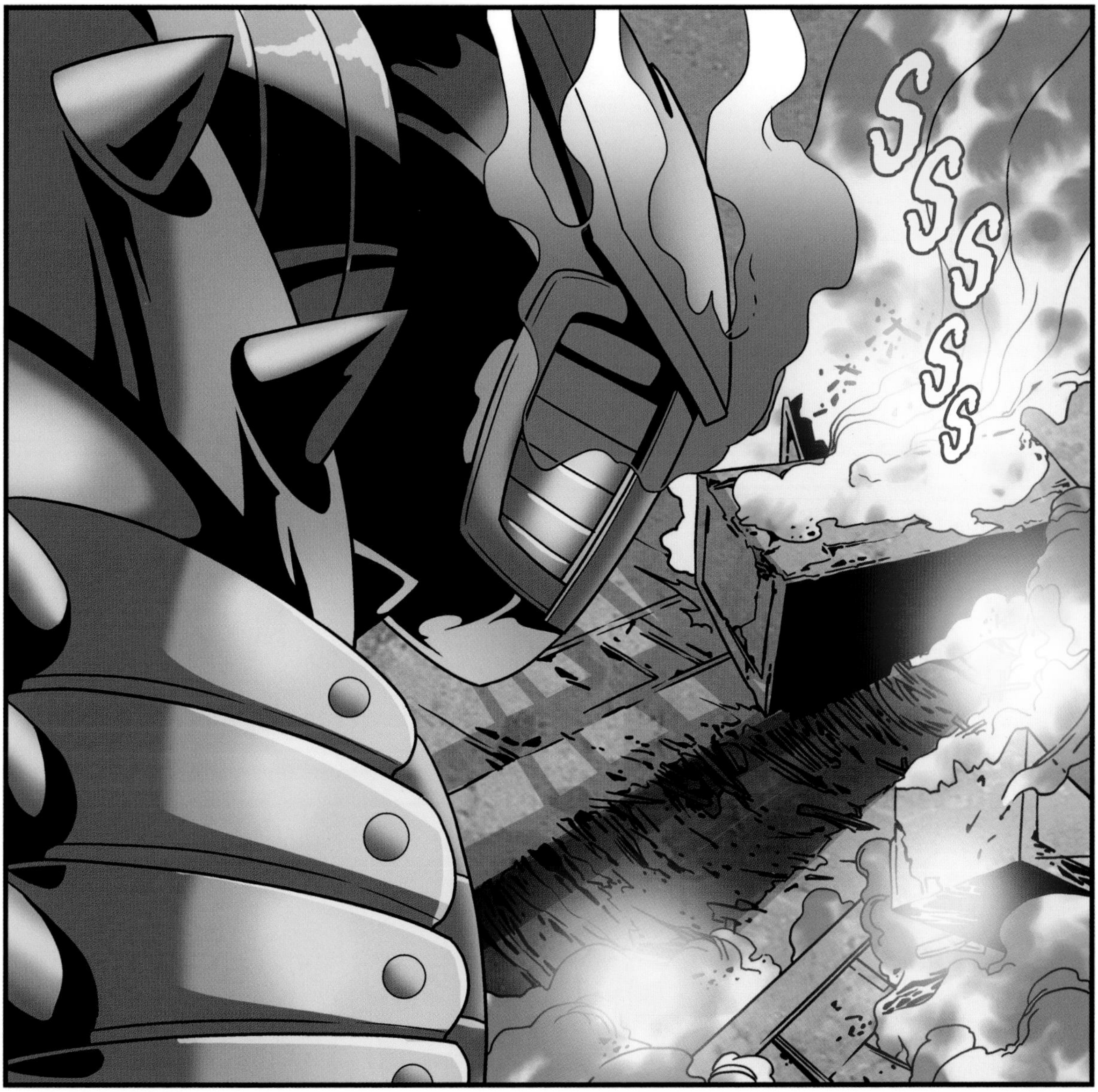
SSSSSSS

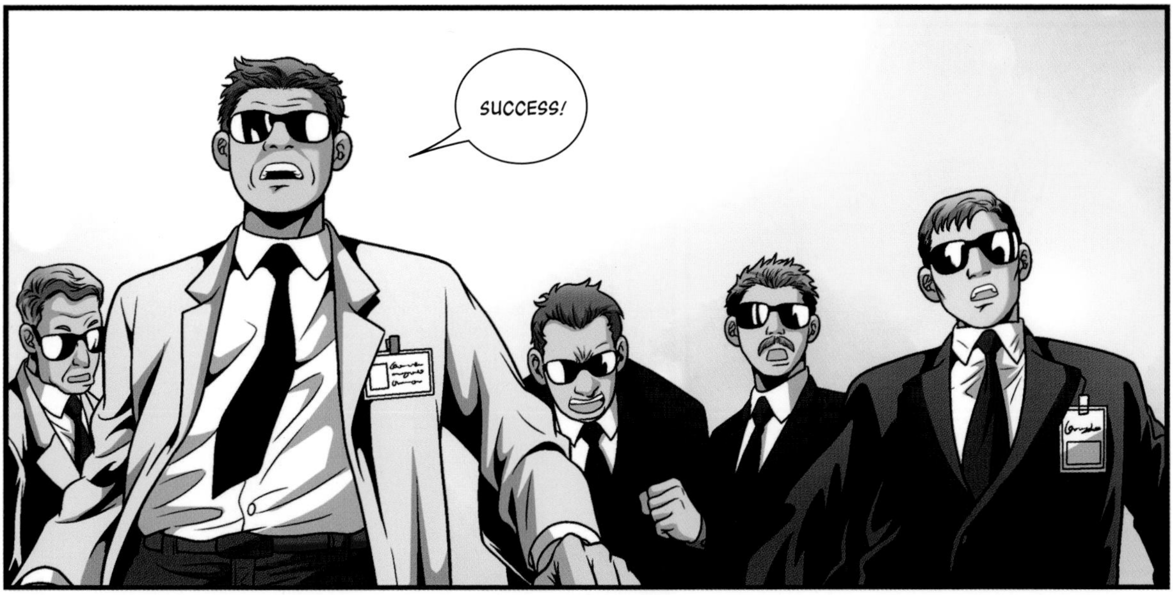
SUCCESS!

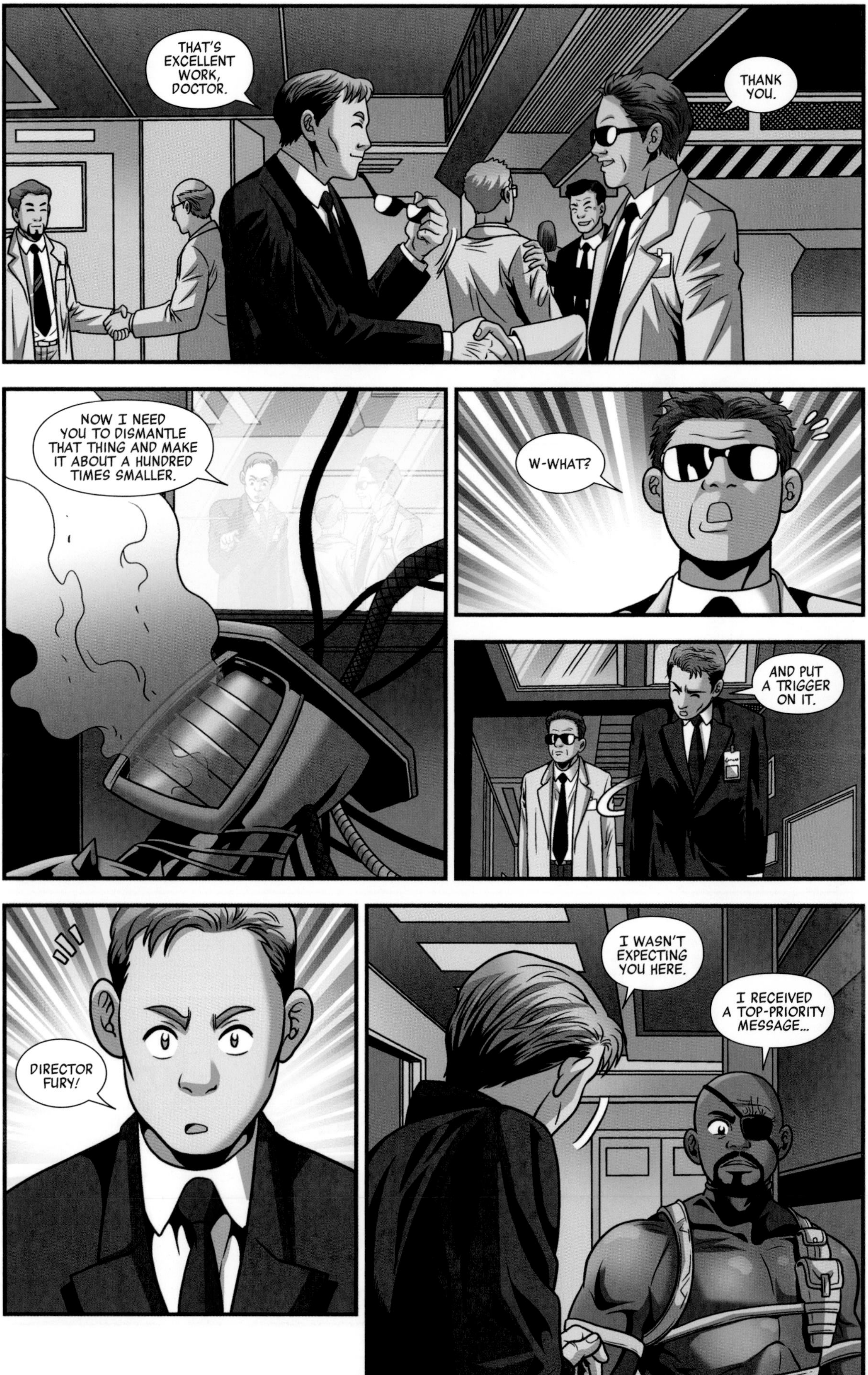
THAT'S EXCELLENT WORK, DOCTOR.
THANK YOU.
NOW I NEED YOU TO DISMANTLE THAT THING AND MAKE IT ABOUT A HUNDRED TIMES SMALLER.
W-WHAT?
AND PUT A TRIGGER ON IT.
DIRECTOR FURY!
I WASN'T EXPECTING YOU HERE.
I RECEIVED A TOP-PRIORITY MESSAGE...

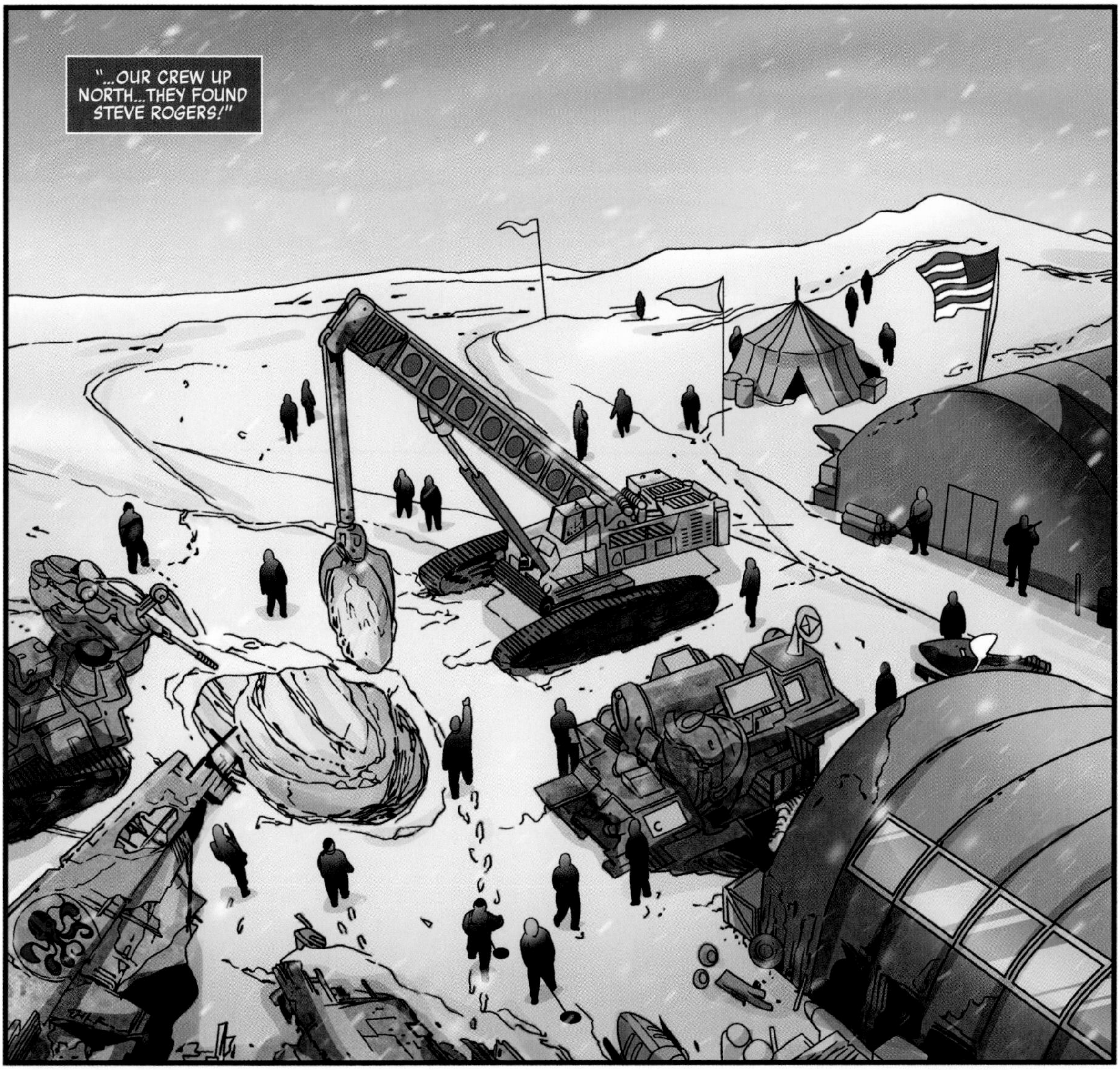
"...OUR CREW UP NORTH...THEY FOUND STEVE ROGERS!"

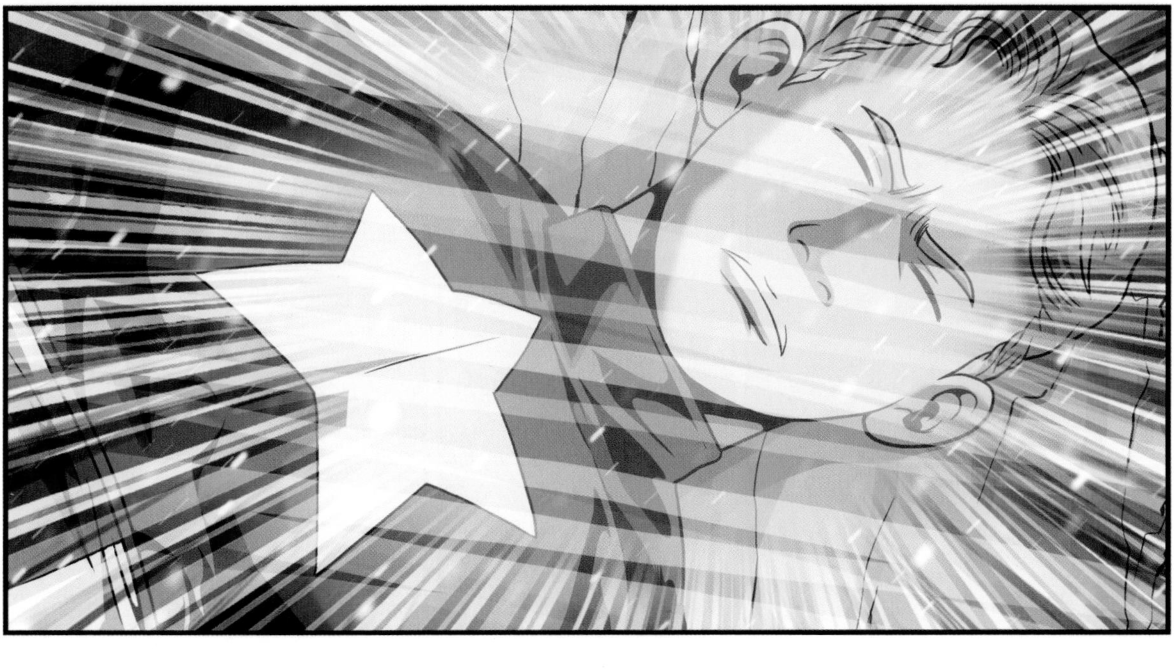

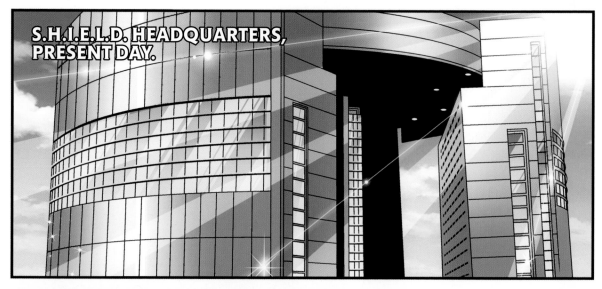

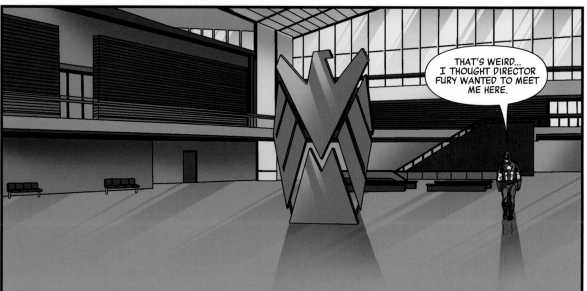

S.H.I.E.L.D. HEADQUARTERS, PRESENT DAY.
THAT'S WEIRD... I THOUGHT DIRECTOR FURY WANTED TO MEET ME HERE.
IS THIS SOME KIND OF TEST?
EVERYTHING'S SO DIFFERENT NOW AND--
RRR...
HUH?!

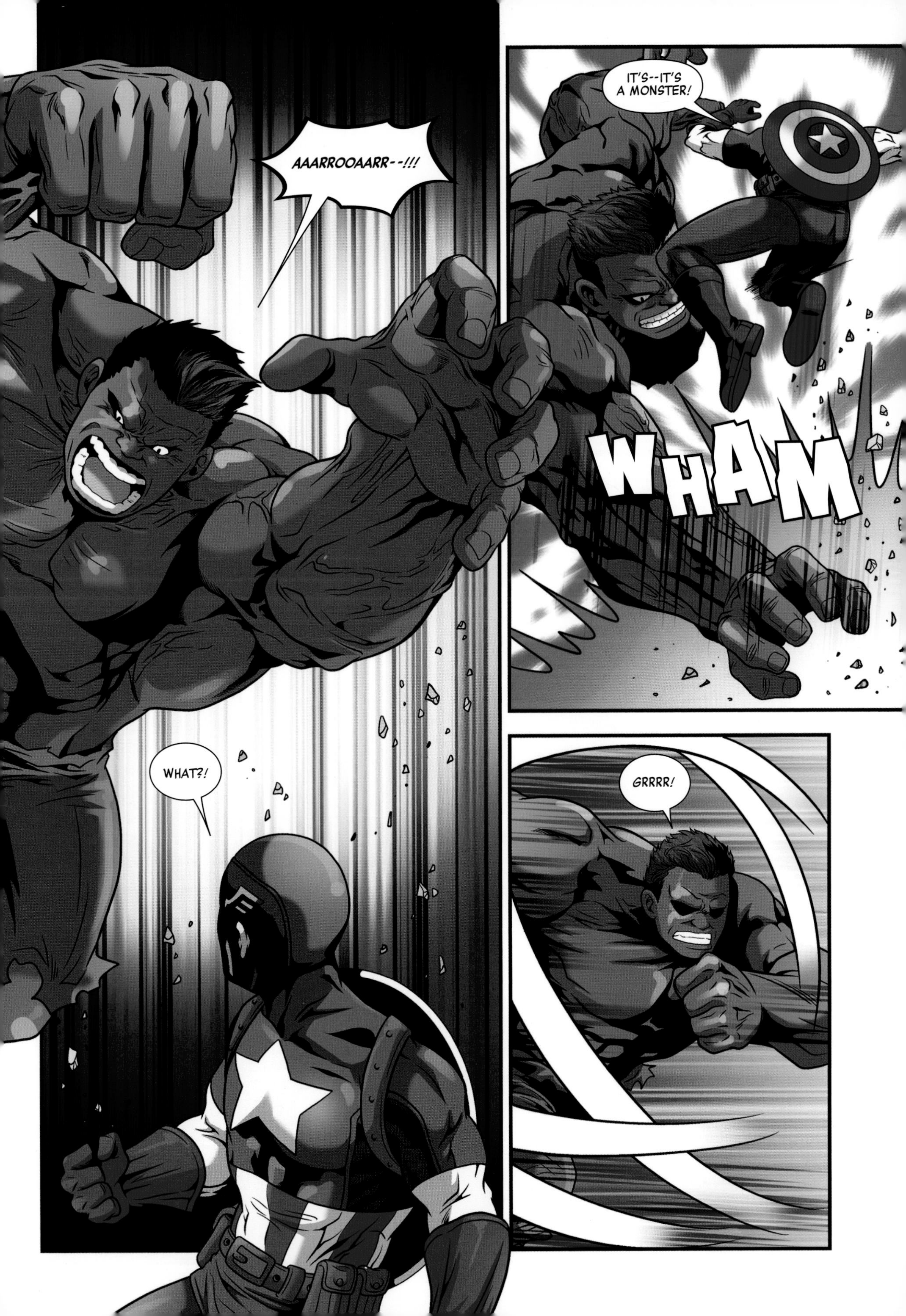
AAARROOAARR--!!!
IT'S--IT'S A MONSTER!
WHAM
WHAT?!
GRRRR!

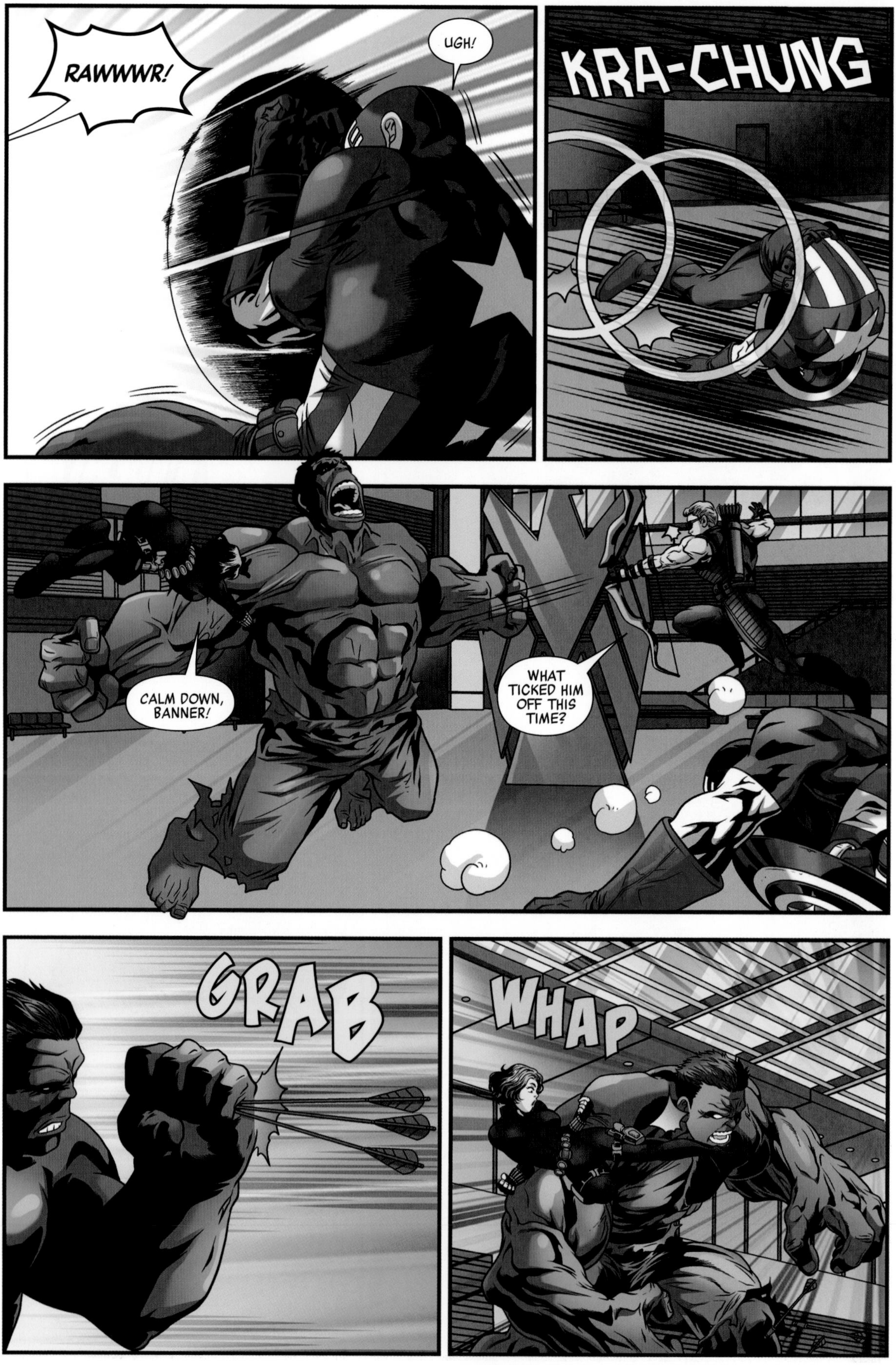
RAWWWR!
UGH!
KRA-CHUNG
CALM DOWN, BANNER!
WHAT TICKED HIM OFF THIS TIME?
GRAB
WHAP

STEP BACK, FOLKS. IRON MAN IS ON THE CASE.

NAY! THIS IS A TASK FOR THE GOD OF THUNDER!

THWAM

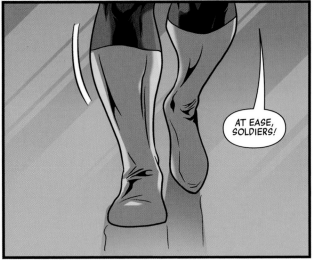

AT EASE, SOLDIERS!

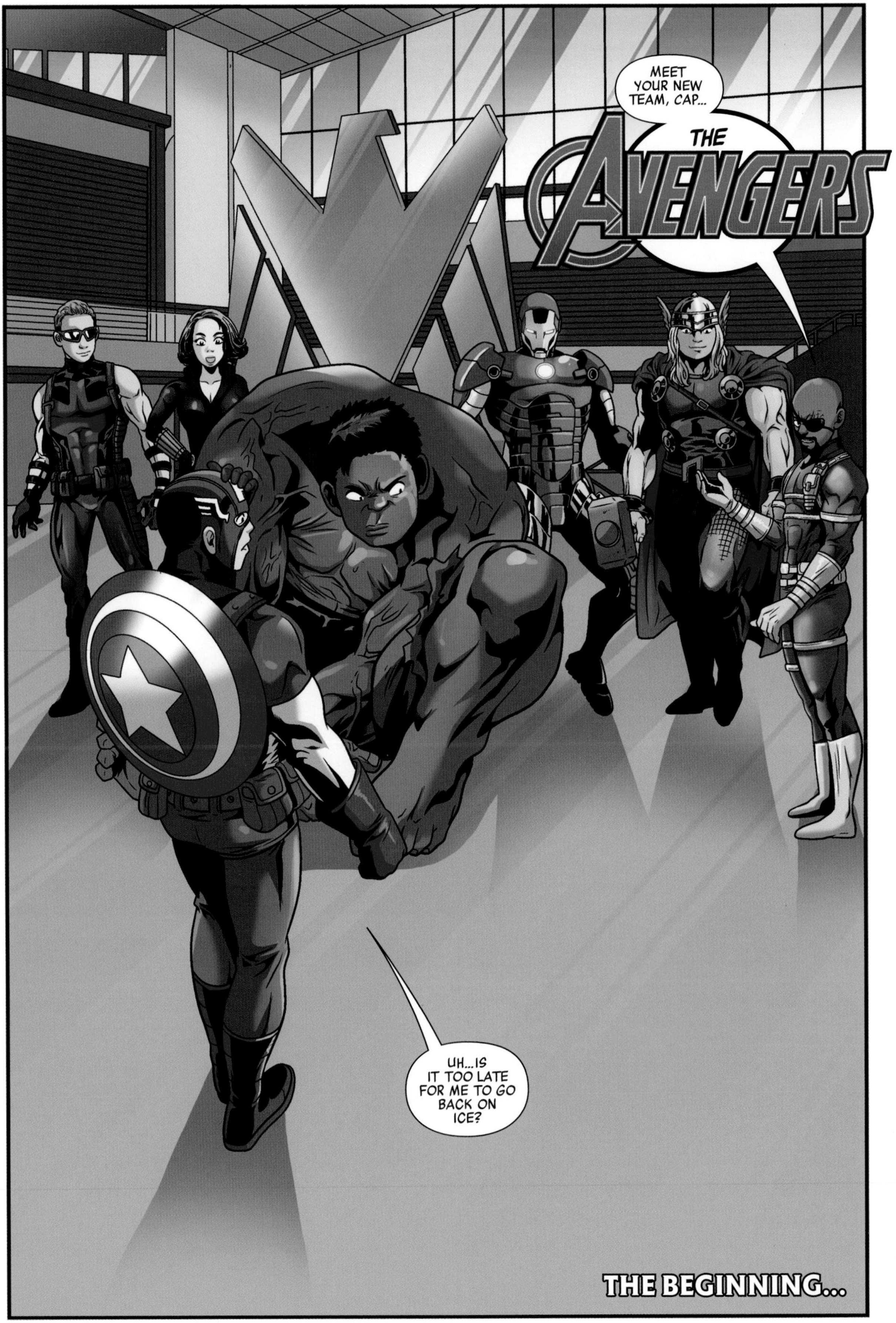
MEET YOUR NEW TEAM, CAP...
THE AVENGERS
UH...IS IT TOO LATE FOR ME TO GO BACK ON ICE?
THE BEGINNING...